BOOK REVIEWS

Here's what people are saying:

. . . the right ingredients for an exciting plot.

from BOSTON GLOBE

A simple, well-written story that will be enjoyed by young readers.

from CHILDREN'S BOOK REVIEW SERVICE

Weekly Reader Books presents

(Original title: The GITTER, The GOOGER & The GHOST)

by Stephen Ryan Oliver

illustrated by Cherie R. Wyman

Carolrhoda Books, Inc. · Minneapolis

This book is a presentation of Weekly Reader Books.
Weekly Reader Books offers book clubs for children
from preschool through high school. For further
information write to: **Weekly Reader Books,**
4343 Equity Drive, Columbus, Ohio 43228.

Published by arrangement with
Carolrhoda Books, Inc.

Cover illustration by David Wenzel.

Manufactured in the United States of America

LIBRARY OF CONGRESS CATALOGING IN PUBLICATION DATA

Oliver, Stephen Ryan.
The Gitter, the Googer, and the ghost.

(The Good time library)
Summary: Ten-year-old best friends and ghost
hunters, known to each other as Gitter and Googer,
think they have a chance to find a real ghost when
Gitter's family inherits an old house in Maine.
[1. Ghosts—Fiction. 2. Maine—Fiction]
I. Wyman, Cherie R., ill. II. Title.
PZ7.0493Gi 1983 [Fic] 83-5281
ISBN 0-87614-250-1 (lib. bdg.)

To my mother, Mary F. Oliver,
To Jimmy, Richard, Neal, Carol, Rita,
Colie, Ann, and Dennis,
To all the "children" in my family for whom
this book was written:
Alan, Scott, Kent, Kathy, Geoff, Susan, Cynthia,
Maureen, David, Mary Lynn, Mike, Rachael,
Ryan, Robbie, Keri, Bridget, Danielle,
Sean, and David,
And to my seventh-grade classes at Hollenbeck
Junior High School in Los Angeles.

A most special thanks to
Susan Pearson, my editor. She knows.

Chapter One

The old Maine house groaned and creaked in protest as the spring storm grew in intensity. A driving rain beat upon the small, old-fashioned window panes; the wind howled eerily and clamored at the doors. A loose shutter somewhere on the second story banged rhythmically.

The house's only occupants, two elderly men, sat in near darkness before a dying fire in the kitchen's large, stone fireplace. The electricity had been out for hours. Neither man flinched at the noise of the storm nor showed any sign of fear that the house that protected them might be harmed by the beating it was taking. In fact, they seemed to pay the storm no attention at all. The old house had weathered much worse than this in its 150 years. So, it seemed, had its occupants.

In appearance the two men were quite different. One of them was dressed in a bulky sweater and suit coat. His round, red face was cleanly shaven. The other wore a plaid flannel shirt, torn at the elbows, beneath his ancient overalls. His eyes twinkled from his craggy, bearded face. Smoke from the curved pipe clenched between his teeth billowed above his head.

There was an ease between the two men that indicated they had known each other for many years, though at the moment the man in the suit coat looked somewhat peeved with his friend. He drummed his fingers on the arm of his chair, then stood up and regarded the bearded man slowly rocking back and forth in a squeaky, old Boston rocker.

"That the way you want it, then?" he asked.

"Ay-yup," answered the bearded man.

"Talk yuh out of it?"

"Nope!"

The clean-shaven man sighed almost inaudibly. "Then I'll see that it's done." He turned and walked to the door. "Good-night."

"Good-bye."

When his friend had left and the man in the rocker was alone in the house, he began to talk softly to himself in a broad, New England accent. The nasal sound of his vowels mingled with the steady creak of his rocking chair and the whistle of the wind to create a bizarre effect: it almost seemed as if the old man were talking to a ghost.

Nearly halfway across the country two young boys were curled up in sleeping bags inside a little pup tent in a backyard telling each other ghost stories. The last thing on their minds was a weathered old house on the coast of Maine.

Chapter Two

Dalton Hornsbee and Prentiss Luggs were best friends and in complete agreement that both of their names were abominable. At the age of six they had made a pact *never* to call each other Dalton or Prentiss, and in the four years that had since passed neither of them had slipped even once. For two of those years, though, they weren't sure just what they *should* call each other. They tried lots of short names, like Dal and Pren, but nothing seemed to please them. Some of their friends called Prentiss "Red" because of his red hair, but that didn't suit them.

What were they supposed to call Dalton, then? Brown? It didn't have much of a ring.

Then one day, when they were eight years old and feeling silly, Prentiss said to Dalton, "Do you know what you look like?"

"What?" asked Dalton.

"You look like a . . . a Gitter!" Prentiss laughed as if he'd said the funniest thing in the whole world, and Dalton laughed too.

"Gitter. Gitter. That's so funny. And you, Prentiss Luggs, look like a . . . a Googer."

The boys could never explain exactly where the names had come from or what they meant, but from that day on everyone except their parents called the two friends the Gitter and the Googer, or Gitter and Googer, or sometimes Git and Goog.

It was spring in Red Wing, Minnesota. The great mounds of snow had melted, the lakes and rivers had shed their winter ice, and the trees were showing lacy, pea-green leaves, while below them the lawns were sprouting new shoots of tender grass through the spring mud. School would be out in less than a month. Winter was finally over!

Red Wing had just been through "one of the worst winters in recorded Minnesota history" according to the television weathermen, but Gitter and Googer had few complaints. Ninety-seven inches of snow between November and March might be a great nuisance for most people, but for Gitter and Googer it had meant a good deal of extra money to be earned by shoveling their neighbors' sidewalks and driveways. It had also meant *six* "snow days" off from school and the most incredible sledding the boys could ever remember. But not even the Gitter and the Googer had liked it very much when it had gotten so cold that they were trapped inside. Googer had counted thirty-two days when the temperature never rose above zero, and on many nights the windchill factor had reached sixty below. It had been out of their boredom during one of those cold spells that the Ghostective Plan had been hatched.

Gitter and Googer had long held plans to go to college together, then open a detective agency in Minneapolis: THE GITTER AND THE GOOGER—PRIVATE EYES. One January day Gitter had suggested that their detective agency specialize in ghost hunting.

"What a great idea," Googer responded, "except that we've never even seen a ghost. How would we know what to look for if someone asked us to hunt one?"

"Practice," said Gitter. "We'll have to practice. We can start with the old Crowly place. There's almost sure to be a ghost *there.*"

The Crowly place had been known to Red Wing children as a haven for boogeymen and witches since Gitter's and Googer's parents had been kids. "It's all nonsense, of course," Mr. Hornsbee had said on more than one occasion. "The Crowlys bought the place as newlyweds, and Mrs. Crowly was pregnant with their first child when Mr. Crowly was killed. Run over by an ice wagon, I think. The child she later gave birth to was retarded, and in those days that was cause for shame. Mrs. Crowly kept the child and herself hidden in that house for the rest of their lives. She didn't even come out after her son died. I guess she was pretty eccentric there at the end, but it was a result of feeling herself an outcast for all those years, not the work of witches. And I'm sure that having all the children who've grown up in the neighborhood over the course of some fifty years chasing through her yard as if the devil himself were after them didn't help her much either."

Mrs. Crowly had died a couple of years ago. The house was an historic landmark and the Historical Society talked of restoring it, but so far they hadn't been able to come up with enough money and the house sat vacant, the lawn overgrown with weeds, the windows gray with dust.

"We can't exactly investigate the Crowly place in this weather," said Googer. "There's at least five feet of snow blocking the doors. Nobody's shoveled there all winter."

"We'll wait for summer then," said Gitter. "Meanwhile, we can do *research*."

And so it was that Dalton Hornsbee and Prentiss Luggs became known—at least to Mrs. Johnson, the town librarian—as Red Wing's leading authorities on ghosts and spirits, or, as the Gitter and the Googer put it, "ghostperts."

It was Saturday morning. Gitter and Googer had spent the night camped out in Gitter's backyard—only the second time they'd been able to sleep out that year. They were hauling their equipment in through the back door when they heard Mrs. Hornsbee gasp, "Good Heavens!" The boys rushed into the living room to find

Gitter's mother standing by the front door with the morning's mail in her hands.

"What's wrong, Mom?"

"Are you all right, Mrs. Hornsbee?"

Mrs. Hornsbee looked up from the letter she was reading. "Oh, yes, I'm quite all right, boys. It's just that we've received the most astonishing letter." Her eyes were wide with wonder. "I can hardly wait to tell Jonathan about it."

That night, after a supper of creamed chicken on baking powder biscuits, Mr. Hornsbee explained the letter to his son while Mrs. Hornsbee called her sister in Minneapolis to tell her the news.

"It seems," said Mr. Hornsbee, lighting his pipe, "that we have—or I should say *had*—a cousin living in the state of Maine. I've never even *heard* of this cousin of ours, one Aloysius Hornsbee, but dog-goned if he didn't up and die."

"How did he die?" asked the Gitter.

"Letter doesn't say, but probably just of old age. He was ninety-one years old."

"Ninety-one! Wow!"

Mr. Hornsbee thought for a moment. "Yes, ninety-one. And I guess he was alone when he died."

"That's kind of sad, isn't it, Dad?"

"Yes, it is, Dalton. It's always sad when someone dies alone. But he had a good, long life—or at least a long one." Mr. Hornsbee fiddled with his pipe for a moment. "His lawyer was instructed to send this letter to us after he died. It seems we are his only heirs."

"Does that mean we're rich?" The Gitter's eyes lit up like street lamps, and visions of living in a great castle with dozens of servants flashed aross his mind.

"I doubt it," said Mr. Hornsbee, smiling. "There's nothing in this letter that would lead me to believe that Aloysius was wealthy, but he did have a rather large house and probably a little money when he passed on."

"And now it belongs to us, right?"

"Well, yes, except there's one little catch.

Cousin Aloysius stated in his will that before we could inherit his estate we had to live in his house for at least one month."

"Wow!" exclaimed the Gitter again. "Are we going to do it? Are we going to go to Maine?"

Mr. Hornsbee lit his pipe again. "We'll see, Dalton. We'll see," he said with a faraway look in his eyes. "Your mother and I haven't really had much of a chance to talk about it yet."

"And now it's time for you to do your homework, then get into bed," said Mrs. Hornsbee, coming into the room.

That night Dalton Hornsbee dreamed of huge castles on high, rocky ridges and of the vast Atlantic Ocean pounding against the rugged coast of Maine. There wasn't a doubt in his mind that Maine would be a far better place to find a ghost than Minnesota was. He could hardly wait to tell Googer.

Chapter Three

A whistle blew out — one, two, three, four — as six twirling batons flew into the air and the drum cadence began, proclaiming the start of the annual Red Wing Memorial Day parade. Just about the entire town was on hand to cheer, and Gitter and Googer had seats right on the curb. The parade was led off by the Red Wing American Legion Post Drum and Bugle Corps, the finest marching band in the state of Minnesota according to Googer's brother Stanley Jr. He played the drums. Gitter and Googer shouted at him as the band thundered and trumpeted its way down the street to the tune of "The Stars and Stripes Forever," but Stanley Jr. either didn't hear them or was ignoring them.

After the parade there was a picnic in the park. It was over the Hornsbees' picnic table, just as the Gitter and the Googer were finishing their old-fashioned spice cake, that Mrs. Hornsbee made this announcement.

"Dalton, your father and I have some news for you," she said. "We have decided that the three of us *will* go to Maine to live in your cousin's house for the summer."

"Yippee!" shouted the Gitter, then immediately felt embarrassed. He'd been hoping that his parents would decide to fulfill the obligations of the will, and he and Googer had spent hours conjecturing about Cousin Aloysius's house and speculating on how many ghosts might live in it, but now that it was coming to pass, Gitter was having second thoughts. One second thought anyway: Googer would be staying in Red Wing. The Gitter looked at the Googer and knew he was thinking the same thing.

"It will be a fabulous adventure," Mr. Hornsbee was saying. "I've arranged for someone to take my summer classes,"—Mr. Hornsbee was a professor—"and I feel as free as a bird. I've never been to Maine, and we'll be living right on the ocean. . . ."

"I'd better get back to my family's table," Googer said softly. As Mr. and Mrs. Hornsbee laughed and talked about the summer ahead, Gitter watched his best friend walk quietly away.

Gitter and Googer had four more days of school following Memorial Day. That left only a little over a week for the Gitter to get ready for his coming adventure. As sad as he was to be leaving Googer behind, he had a lot to do to keep his mind off it. As for Googer, the summer ahead looked pretty bleak without his best friend, but he was determined to make sure that Gitter was prepared for all possibilities when he arrived in Maine.

The Hornsbees were to leave on June 11. On June 9, the Googer arrived at their house with a huge box for the Gitter. The boys carried it up to Gitter's room.

"If you're going to find a ghost," said Googer sheepishly, "you'll need to be able to get around after dark." He pulled out his super-duper Spiderman flashlight—the one he had gotten only last Christmas. "So you better take this along."

"Wow! Thanks," said the Gitter. "But won't you be needing this?"

"Naw, I figured we would have needed it if we went ghost hunting up at the old Crowly place, but I'm not going alone. You take it," Googer said as he next pulled out a yellow, rubber raincoat.

"What's that?" asked Gitter.

"My dad calls it a slicker, but my mom calls it a mackintosh." Googer held it up, then flopped a round, banana-colored hat on his friend's head and laughed. "Now you're all set for the ocean storms."

The Gitter put on the coat and looked into his mirror. The coat and hat were both a little big for him.

"I look just like that boy in the commercial for fish sticks," he said.

Googer faked a deep voice like the one on the TV commercial and sang, "Gorton's of Gloucester," then asked, "And what do *you* do, young man?"

"I'm a stick fisherman," Gitter replied.

"You mean you fish with a stick?" Googer questioned.

"Nope. I mean I catch fish sticks."

The boys laughed. They were really going to miss each other.

Googer's parents invited the Hornsbees over for dinner on the night before they were to leave for Maine. The Luggs lived only three blocks away from the Hornsbees, but sometimes Gitter thought it was almost as if Googer lived on another planet.

The difference was that Gitter lived with only his parents, while Googer lived in a whole houseful of people. Three brothers, two sisters, his mother and dad, and his grandmother, plus Googer himself of course, all lived in one big raucous house. Sometimes Gitter was just a little bit jealous, especially over Googer's grandmother. She even called him Googer instead of Prentiss. Googer called her Granny Goodwich.

Granny Goodwich was a feisty little woman with bright red hair—just a shade brighter than the rest of the Luggs family, since "I have to mask this gray mop with a little something else, and it never comes out exactly right," she said. "Red is tricky."

The nine Luggs and the three Hornsbees gathered around the enormous dining-room table. As they sat down, Gitter noticed a strange smile on Granny Goodwich's lips and an extra sparkle in her lively blue eyes. Gitter looked at the others, then back at Granny. It seemed to him as if she was sharing a secret with everyone at the table except Googer and him.

"All right, everyone," said Granny Goodwich, "before we eat, it's time for a little Christmas." In her hands she held a small green box tied with a shiny red ribbon.

"Christmas?" said the Gitter and the Googer together, quizzical frowns on their faces. Everyone else was smiling.

"Sometimes we need a little Christmas even on a warm June evening when the lilacs are in bloom," Granny said as she handed the package to her grandson. "Here, Googer. Merry Christmas from all of us."

The boys had no idea what was going on.

"For me?" Googer said. "I don't get it."

"Just open the box, Prentiss," said Mrs. Luggs, smiling.

Everyone's eyes were on Googer as he opened the box and pulled out an envelope. It took him a little while to figure out what the papers inside the envelope were, but the Gitter knew right away. It was an airline ticket—round trip from Min-

neapolis-St. Paul to Boston, Massachusetts.

There was so much excitement in the air that no one wanted to break it by speaking, but finally Gitter broke the silence.

"You're coming with us!" he shouted. "I can't believe it! It's fantastic!"

Everyone laughed and clapped, but Googer just sat there with his mouth wide open and his eyes glowing.

"Aren't you going to say something, Prentiss?" asked his father.

"Speech! Speech!" cried Sally Luggs, then everyone joined in with the cry.

Googer stood, held up the ticket in one hand, threw his other arm around Gitter's shoulder, and hollered, "The Gitter and the Googer ride again!"

Chapter Four

Moody, Maine, sits right on the Atlantic about seventy miles north of Boston, a quaint little town that somehow seems lost in time. Its houses are almost all small wooden structures, many of them over 100 years old and a few much older than that. Its main street has a number of little shops and businesses, a post office, two churches, and an old-fashioned general store.

Everywhere in Moody there is evidence of what the people who live there do for a living—they fish the Atlantic, mostly for that traditional Maine delicacy, lobster.

A small office over Sanger's Drug Store on Main Street was the business address of the town's only lawyer, Mr. Orly Bean (of the Massachusetts Beans). Orly had been practicing law for nearly fifty years, forty of them in Moody. He was soft-spoken and rosy-cheeked, a man of general good nature. On June 11, however, Orly Bean was feeling neither soft-spoken nor good-natured.

"Dog blast it, Ashton! Where's that airline schedule for the Hornsbees?" he bellowed from behind his massive oak desk.

Ken Ashton, a young law student up from Boston, was working for Mr. Bean for the summer.

"It's in my pocket, Mr. Bean," said the smiling, blond-haired man.

"Shouldn't you be on your way to Boston to pick them up?"

Ken looked at his wristwatch.

"I believe they're just taking off from Minneapolis now, Mr. Bean. They won't be landing in Boston for another three hours. Boston is only..."

"I know how far away Boston is, but I don't want you to be late. Now move it!"

Mr. Bean really liked Ken and appreciated his help, but today Bean was edgy.

"I'm on my way, Mr. Bean," Ken said, looking directly at his boss. It was easy to tell when Orly shouldn't be argued with: his round, red face got even redder and he nervously drummed his fingers on any surface he found close at hand.

Alone in his office, Orly Bean muttered to himself. "Dog blast it, Aloysius Hornsbee, why did you have to complicate my life with this goofy will. Now I'll be stuck with those kin of yours from Minnesota all summer. Of all the darn fool things I ever heard of...."

Orly's thoughts were interrupted by the ringing of his telephone. He sighed and picked up the receiver.

"Hello, Orly Bean here.... Oh, it's you. ...No, no.... He just left a minute ago."

Orly began to drum his fingers on the desk again.

All thoughts of the ghost that Gitter and Googer fully expected to find in Maine temporarily vanished the moment the boys caught their first glimpse of the magnificent machine that was to carry them to Boston. A 747, the inside of the airplane was as big as the Cinema Three movie theater in Red Wing, or so it seemed to Gitter and Googer as they boarded their "first ever" airplane. They could hardly believe that this giant was actually going to fly.

As the four engines of the 747 each delivered their 50,000 pounds of thrust to lift Gitter, Googer, the Hornsbees, and 350 tons of people and machine into the air, the boys were dumbfounded. Even Mr. and Mrs. Hornsbee, who had flown several times before, couldn't help but be impressed.

When the captain announced that passengers were now free to move about the cabin, Googer unbuckled his seatbelt and joined Gitter in pressing his nose to the window.

"Wow," Gitter breathed.

"Flying is FAN-tastic," said Googer.

The flight was smooth and easy most of the way to Boston, the plane cruising along at 600 miles per hour, 35,000 feet in the air, the Gitter and the Googer having the time of their lives. When the stewardess stopped to explain to them the noises they would be hearing when the plane prepared for landing at Logan Airport, the two friends couldn't believe that the three-hour flight was already coming to an end.

The plane made a wide arc and flew out over the ocean before swooping down and lowering its landing gear. Gitter and Googer pressed their faces to the little windows, ignoring the funny feeling in their stomachs as the plane dropped lower over the coastline. Soon the runways of

Logan Airport were in view and the seat-belt sign went on. Then, like a huge, fat duck, the jet touched down on the ground, skimmed the runway, reversed its engines with an enormous roar, and slowed to a crawl. The Gitter and the Googer were in Boston.

Chapter Five

"On the coast of Maine, where green islands and salt inlets fringe the deep-cut shoreline; where balsam firs and bayberry bushes send their fragrance far seaward, and song sparrows sing all day, and the tide runs splashing in and out among the weedy ledges; where cow-bells tinkle on the hills and herons stand in the shady coves—on the lonely coast of Maine stood a small gray house facing the morning light. All the weather-beaten houses of that region face the sea apprehensively, like the women who live in them."

—Sarah Orne Jewett, Maine, 1896

"It's so picturesque, I can hardly believe

it," said Mrs. Hornsbee as Ken drove them up the Atlantic coast to Moody. Gitter and Googer kept their eyes peeled for glimpses of the formidable granite coastline and were occasionally treated with scenes of awesome beauty and majesty. By the time they arrived in town, the sun had begun to dip into the western horizon.

Orly Bean met the group at his office. After going over some details with Mr. and Mrs. Hornsbee, he said goodnight to Ken Ashton and took the rest of the group to the Grotto Restaurant on Main Street for a dinner of fresh Maine lobster and boiled new potatoes. Gitter and Googer had never eaten whole lobster before and were thoroughly pleased at having to use nutcrackers to get to the meat.

Mr. Bean seemed a little nervous and officious at first, but when the boys began asking him questions about the house and the town, he perked right up and interrupted his slow speech only to take bites of his lobster. Everyone reveled in his quaint stories and enjoyed the funny way his words sounded. "Ay-yup," he would say instead of "Yes." And all his vowels, but especially the As, seemed a lot longer than they sounded in Minnesota.

Some of his tales were as spooky as the ghost stories with which Gitter and Googer loved to scare each other.

"No tale is stranger, though, than that of *The Curse of Squando,*" Orly Bean said as he sipped on a cup of steaming black coffee. "In 1675, just a couple of miles north of here on the Saco River, a bunch of drunken Englishmen wanted to test out some crazy theory that Indians, even babies, were natural swimmers. So they set about along the river and tipped over a canoe which carried an Indian woman and her baby. She was able to save the child from the waters of the Saco, but later it died from the effects of the chill. Ay-yup, and the father of that baby was Squando, Chief of the Sokoki Indians. The grief-stricken father and his braves took to the warpath, and the towns of Biddleford and Saco went up in flames that night. Then Squando cursed the river. He swore it would take three lives a year, and from that time on three lumbermen, or fishermen, or swimmers died in the Saco each year. Between 1676 and 1878 more than 600 people drowned there." He paused for emphasis, then concluded, "Ay-yup. Victims of *The Curse of Squando*."

The boys had all but forgotten their dinners as they listened raptly to Orly Bean. Mr. and Mrs. Hornsbee enjoyed the stories too, despite the fact that Mr. Hornsbee's occasional wink in the direction of Mr. Bean failed to produce from him anything but a look of steadfast belief in the tales he was telling.

"I think he actually believes this stuff," Gitter heard his father whisper to his mother.

"What happened after 1878?" Googer asked.

"Yes," Gitter chimed in. "Did the curse stop?"

"Waall," Mr. Bean said, "the drownings did slow down a mite, but they didn't stop completely until 1928."

"I wonder why they stopped," Gitter mused.

"Perhaps the curse was fulfilled," Bean answered. "Perhaps it'll start again. Who knows?"

The boys looked at each other and shuddered.

"Your cousin Aloysius is more knowledgeable about supernatural matters than most anyone in these parts." Orly Bean drummed his fingers on the table and looked right at the Gitter.

"But he's dead," both of the boys said at the same time.

Bean stammered a bit, suddenly looking like the old man he was. "Yes. Dead." He paused. "Your cousin was a dear friend of mine. Sometimes I forget he's gone." He cleared his throat. "Aloysius loved the tales and legends of Maine. He could raise the hair on your neck with the story of the Windingo."

"Tell us that one," said Googer, but Mr. Hornsbee interrupted before Bean could begin.

"I think we should get to the house and get settled in, Mr. Bean."

"Aw, Dad," protested Gitter.

"We appreciate your kindness and your strange stories," Mr. Hornsbee continued, "but perhaps they're a little *too* strange for two young boys who have never spent a night away from Red Wing, Minnesota."

"Ay-yup," Orly answered and signaled to the waitress for the check.

The house stood alone on a cliff above the rocky shoreline. It was an old house, built over 150 years ago, Bean had told them. But like the men who had built it, the Hornsbee house was rugged and solid.

Although it was dark when Mr. Bean turned off the two-lane road into the driveway, the broad outlines of the big, two-story, squarish building with its gray, weather-beaten, wooden siding and pronounced chimneys stood out in the moonlight in dramatic relief. The trim around the tiny, criss-crossed window panes was a bright, shiny white, glistening with the mist that rose from the ocean below.

"Well, this is it," Orly Bean said. "You have the keys and the instructions. Ashton brought your bags out, so you're all set."

"Thank you, Mr. Bean," Mrs. Hornsbee said. "We'll be just fine."

"Ay-yup. I believe you will."

Mr. and Mrs. Hornsbee, Gitter, and Googer wearily got out of Bean's car and stood looking at what would be their home for the summer. A cool breeze blew their hair about their curious faces as they stood before the house. Orly Bean backed the car down the gravel drive. Before they could get to the door, however, Bean stopped his car, got out, and called back to the new occupants.

"Just remember... Aloysius Hornsbee loved this house, as did his father, and *his* father before him. It's not a good idea to disturb the . . ." Bean's words faded into the wind.

"Don't worry, Mr. Bean. Don't worry," Jonathan Hornsbee answered as they watched Mr. Bean drive away.

"I wonder what his game is," Mr. Hornsbee said to his wife as they went inside. "I'd swear he was trying to spook us."

Cynthia Hornsbee laughed. "He almost *did* spook me. I'll be afraid to go swimming for a month."

The inside of the house was as warm and cozy as the outside had been chilly and damp. A big fire, compliments of Ken Ashton, burned in the main room downstairs. There was also a fire in the kitchen fireplace and a surprising number of supplies in the cupboards—even a carton of milk and a dozen eggs in the refrigerator.

"Wasn't that thoughtful of Mr. Bean," said Mrs. Hornsbee. "And just look at this kitchen. I love it!"

The kitchen was enormous and thoroughly old-fashioned, complete with an old wood stove, a vintage refrigerator, and a big kitchen table. The table and chairs looked as if they'd been painted a hundred times.

"Boy! This is just like something in the movies," Gitter said in awe. "Everything is so *old*."

Mrs. Hornsbee laughed. "Some of these things aren't *that* old. I can remember having a wood stove at home when I was your age. How about a cup of cocoa before bed?"

The Googer was looking out a window in the front room. "Hey, Gitter!" he called out. "Look down there!"

Gitter ran to his friend and peered out into the darkness. Nestled among the granite rocks about a quarter of a mile up the coast was a lighthouse. The boys couldn't make out much detail in the darkness, but since no light came from it, they assumed the lighthouse must no longer be in use.

"There'll be plenty of time to see everything tomorrow," Mr. Hornsbee said as he too squinted out the window for a glimpse of the old lighthouse. "Right now you two travelers had better get ready for bed."

There were two staircases leading to the upper floor, one from the kitchen and one from the front room. Upstairs they found their bags in their bedrooms, Mr. and Mrs. Hornsbee's in the large master bedroom near the front of the house, the boys' in the twin-bedded room near the rear.

The boys changed into their pajamas and curled up under down comforters that felt surprisingly good this June night. Mrs. Hornsbee brought up three mugs of cocoa. She sat with them for a few minutes, then lightly kissed them each goodnight and went to bed herself.

Googer lay in bed thinking. "Boy, Git," he said after a time, "the old Crowly place is *nothing* compared to this. We're gonna find some ghost *here*!"

A light snore was his only answer.
"Ay-yup," Googer answered himself.

Chapter Six

The next few days were just about perfect as far as the Gitter and the Googer were concerned. The possibilities for exploration seemed endless, and catching a ghost got put on a back burner for a bit.

The first item on their agenda was to climb down the long, rickety, wooden staircase that led to the rocky beach below. Gitter and Googer spent hours down there as pirates, fishermen, spies, or just walking the shore looking for stranded starfish and listening to the pounding of the breakers. Mr. Hornsbee laid down the law about the lighthouse, though: Under no circumstances were the boys to step foot on the causeway that led out to it without him along, and he didn't have time for that right now. The Hornsbee yard was in proportion to the house—large—and both lawn and shrubbery were in need of his immediate attention.

Mrs. Hornsbee, too, was busy. A garden plot took up one corner of the lot and she was wasting no time in turning it over and getting some seeds planted. She enlisted the boys' help to clean out a strawberry patch—tedious work, but the promise of fresh strawberries to come made it worth the effort. Mr. Hornsbee reported that there would also be blueberries for the taking later in the summer from a nearby woods where he had gone to dump some grass cuttings.

In another corner of the lot was a cluster of apple trees. Their blossoms were falling now, but the sweet smell lingered and made tree climbing irresistible. A two-story garage proved irresistible as well, yielding all sorts of good stuff—a tire and some rope with which to make a tree swing in the giant oak beside the house, plenty of scrap lumber and tools to build a platform high up in the same tree, and, best of all, a trunk full of old nautical equipment including a compass, a brass barometer, and an ancient spyglass.

From their platform in the oak the boys spied on the activities of the folks of Moody, Maine. It was a quiet town for the most part, but twice a day it sprang to life—early in the morning when the fishermen prepared to take their boats out, and late in the afternoon when they returned. Gitter and Googer often walked down to the harbor to watch. They were particularly fascinated with the lobster traps—strange contraptions that looked like barrels made of slats, then cut in half lengthwise.

The boys were under instructions not to bother any of the busy men, but one morning as they were watching, a crusty, old lobsterman looked up from loading his traps and stared at them.

"Seen yuh boys down here afore," he finally said.

"We're living here for the summer," Googer offered.

"Yuh aren't Down Easters, now, are yuh?"

The boys looked at each other, not understanding the question.

"Nope. I guess yuh not," the man said as he continued with his traps.

"What's a Down Easter?" Gitter asked.

The lobsterman didn't answer, but continued his work until the last trap was hauled onto his boat. Gitter and Googer were a bit embarrassed by his silence and turned to leave the dock.

"Now, boys," the deep voice said, "if yuh goin' to live about here, yuh best know that a Down Easter is what we folks who live here in Maine call ourselves."

"Oh." Gitter nodded.

"Where yuh boys living?" The man squinted at them in the bright sunshine.

"Up there," Googer said and pointed in the direction of the Hornsbee house.

"Up there? Yuh live in a tree?"

Gitter was annoyed. "We live in the Hornsbee house," he answered firmly. "I'm called Gitter, and this is my best friend, Googer."

"So you're Aloysius's kin," the strange man said, arching one bushy eyebrow.

"Did you know my cousin?" Gitter asked.

"In a manner of speaking, I still do," the man answered.

"But he's dead," the boys said.

"Aye, boys. But old lobstermen never die, they just shut their traps." The man laughed heartily at his joke. "Yuh see, boys," he said more ominously, "a lobsterman kin never rest in peace till every trap he's ever set is hauled in."

Googer looked directly into the old man's weathered face. Was he making a joke? He hesitated, then asked, "Does Aloysious still have traps set?"

The lobsterman pulled a crooked, old

pipe from his shirt pocket, put one foot up on the edge of the boat, and whispered conspiratorially, "Only one that I know of."

Googer shivered.

The Hornsbee house squeaked and groaned and rattled at night, especially when the wind was up. Its doors creaked on rusty hinges and latches, its windows rattled like old bones, and its planked floors seemed to protest the weight of 150 years of walkers.

The night after Gitter and Googer met the strange lobsterman, a storm began to brew. Thunder rolled in from the west, quietly at first, like a cat purring. The Gitter and the Googer had been in their beds for over an hour but were still wide awake.

"That old man gave me the willies," Googer confessed.

"He was just kidding around with us, Goog," said the Gitter. "I liked him."

A window separated the twin beds. In

spite of the cool nights, the boys usually kept it open so they could listen to the low, comforting roar of the ocean. Tonight, however, they listened to other things. "Cuh-lick . . . cuh-lick," the door to their room sounded as the breeze pulled it slightly open, then pushed it back to touch the broken latch. Googer got up and shut the window. As the storm picked up, the wind rattled the panes. Then the thunder began to roar a little louder, and the ocean crashed against the rocks below the house.

"Gitter, did you hear something?" whispered the Googer.

"Of course, I hear a lot of things. It's just the storm and this old house. Let's go to sleep."

"*You* go to sleep. I think there's something in this house, and I'm going to find out what. We're ghostectives, remember?"

Googer slipped out of his bed, found his Spiderman flashlight, and was out of the bedroom before Gitter could protest. He shined the thin beam up and down the narrow hallway, then headed down the back stairway to the kitchen. The smell of the woodstove still hung in the darkened room, and the wind knocked heavy beads of rain against the window panes. Barefoot, Googer stepped onto the cold kitchen floor. A chill ran all the way up his back to his neck. He let his flashlight beam play about the kitchen—over the table where they had eaten supper, the Boston rocker, the stone fireplace, the basement door. Sounds of footsteps seemed to be coming from behind that door, barely rising above the noise of the storm. Or was it just the wind rattling some loose board? No, Googer was certain he heard footsteps on the basement stairs. His stomach churned. He backed away from the door. His mouth grew dry and coppery tasting. He was certain he could see the iron doorknob slowly turn. His breath stopped. Heart pounding, he took another step backward.

"Yeow!" he screamed as his pajama-clad

bottom touched the still smoldering wood stove. The flashlight flew into the air and crashed onto the floor. Googer made a beeline for the back stairs, taking them two at a time even in the darkness. Halfway up something grabbed his arm.

"Shhh! You're going to wake the whole house." It was the Gitter.

Once they were safely back in their room, Googer told Gitter of the footsteps on the basement stairs.

"It's just the storm, Goog."

"No, it wasn't," Googer insisted. "Someone was coming up the basement stairs."

A hall window must have been open, for suddenly a huge gust of wind forced the boys' bedroom door crashing against the wall. The thunder clapped so loudly, it sounded as if the earth itself was blowing apart. For a brief, terrifying instant, a flash of lightning illuminated the darkened room.

There in the doorway stood a ghost more horrifying than either the Gitter or the

Googer would ever have imagined.

"It was horrible, Dad," said the Gitter. "It was a great big man with an awful, wrinkled face..."

"...and a white beard sort of low on his chin and around his cheeks," interrupted Googer, "but no moustache."

It had taken only a few seconds for the boys' screams to bring Mr. Hornsbee into the room.

"And his eyes," the Gitter added, "his eyes were so evil looking."

Mr. Hornsbee frowned. "If you did see this man, what makes you think it was a ghost?"

Googer didn't hesitate with his answer. "Because one minute he was there, and the next minute he was gone. He just disappeared."

"You didn't see anything in the hall, did you, Dad?"

"No. No, I didn't, but..."

Just then Mrs. Hornsbee came into the

bedroom. "I've checked the doors, Jonathan. They're both locked."

"I think Gitter and Googer here just have a bad case of thunderstorm imagination," said Gitter's father.

"Dad!" "Mr. Hornsbee!" the boys protested.

"Why don't we all go back to bed. We'll talk about this in the morning," Mrs. Hornsbee suggested.

"Good idea, honey. Boys, I'll leave the lamp on the desk turned on if you like," Mr. Hornsbee said, and he and his wife left the room.

Googer got up, turned off the lamp, and crawled back into his bed.

"We did see it, didn't we?" Gitter asked in the darkness.

"We sure did.... Are you still scared?"

"No. I don't think ghosts come back twice in the same night."

"Boy, Git, this is really something, huh?"

"Ay-yup," answered Gitter. "Looks like we're going to catch our first ghost this summer for sure!"

The storm had passed out to sea and the house was quiet. At last the two boys fell asleep, but their dreams were filled with the ghost. In the Gitter's dream the ghost was huge. He beckoned Gitter down a staircase that seemed miles long and ended up not in the basement but in the sea. Although Gitter didn't want to do it, some force compelled him to walk down the thousands of steps until briny water splashed about his feet and he was being pulled deeper and deeper into the ocean.

Googer's ghost resembled the sea god, Neptune. "Help me. . . . Help me," the ghost-god was mouthing silently. Then one gigantic arm lifted a string of miniature lobster traps from the icy water and the ghost leaned down to Googer and whispered, "No lobsterman can ever rest in peace till every trap he's ever set has been hauled in." Then the ghost took on the appearance of the strange old fisherman the boys had talked to in the harbor. He laughed a hollow laugh and held the traps close to Googer's face. In each of them was a little Gitter and a little Googer struggling to get out.

When the boys told each other their dreams the next morning, they discovered that although their dreams had been distinctly different, one thing was the same in each. In the background of both dreams had been the unmistakable sound of old-fashioned fiddle music.

Chapter Seven

After breakfast Gitter and Googer decided to walk along their favorite part of the beach. It was a foggy morning, and before they knew it, they had reached the point where the causeway ran out to the old lighthouse.

"Look," said Googer, pointing through the fog. "There's someone standing out by the lighthouse."

"I don't see anyone," Gitter replied.

"He must have gone around to the other side. Let's go look."

"You know the lighthouse is off limits."

"I know, but..." Before Googer could

think of an excuse, the figure appeared out of the fog again and started walking toward them. There was something eerie about the man walking through the mist. His feet were clearly visible, but his torso and face were clouded in fog.

Gitter and Googer looked at each other with the same question in their eyes: Should they run?

"Who's there?" the voice from the fog bellowed out. The boys didn't answer as it soon became apparent that the man was the old fisherman they had talked to down at the harbor, and they figured he could see them now too. "Aye, if it isn't Gitter and Googer."

"Yes, sir," Googer answered. "It's us."

"Yuh warn't plannin' on goin' out to the lighthouse, were yuh?"

"Oh, no, sir. My father says that's off limits to us," Gitter said.

"Smart man, yuh father. Ay-yup. Comin' down to the harbor today?"

"Maybe," said Gitter.

"Well, if yuh do, stop by the boat. I'll be workin' on her the best part of the day most likely. Or if I'm not there, just ask around for Benjamin Whittle."

The old man turned and set off down the beach toward town, soon disappearing in the fog.

"What do you suppose he was doing out there?" Gitter asked.

"I don't know, but I'd like to find out," Googer said. In the fog the lighthouse looked even more mysterious than usual, and now that Benjamin Whittle had, in a manner, warned them not to go out to it, they were even more curious.

The boys resisted temptation, though, and headed instead back to the long staircase that led up from the beach to the Hornsbee house. The fog was thicker now, and only a dim outline of the house was visible above them.

Gitter and Googer went into the kitchen where Mr. and Mrs. Hornsbee sat drinking coffee and reading the newspaper.

"I'm glad to see you boys didn't get lost in this fog," said Mrs. Hornsbee.

"We were walking down by the old lighthouse when we saw..."

"Hey, Gitter, look at this!" Googer interrupted. He'd been rummaging in a kitchen drawer and had pulled out an old, yellowed photograph.

"Holy cow!" Gitter gasped. "That's him—the ghost we saw last night!"

Mr. Hornsbee examined the photograph. "This *is* an old one," he said with admiration in his voice. On the back was written, *D. Hornsbee, 1814-1899.* "Aloysius's grandfather, probably. Are you boys sure you've never seen this picture before?"

"I never have," Gitter answered.

"Me neither," Googer added. "But I've seen that man before—*last night*!"

"Shhh. Be quiet!" Gitter said.

"What do you mean, be..."

"Just listen. Don't you hear it?" said Gitter.

The four of them strained their ears,

and, sure enough, though faint at first, the sound of fiddle music could be heard. For a moment they all listened to the scratchy strains of some sea ditty.

"I've heard that before," whispered Googer.

Gitter nodded. "Me too. Last night in my dreams."

"Someone is obviously trying to spook us," said an irritated Mr. Hornsbee, "but maybe now we'll get to the bottom of all this ghost nonsense. It sounds to me like the music is coming from the basement."

Mr. Hornsbee opened the basement door, but the music stopped the instant he did so. Carefully he led the Gitter, the Googer, and Mrs. Hornsbee down the rickety stairs into the cellar darkness. He fumbled around for the light switch only to find that the bulb was burned out, but before he could call a halt to the search, Googer had retrieved his Spiderman flashlight from the kitchen where he'd left it in his panic the night before. Its narrow beam

RAHY'S
EN STRIKE

showed them a dingy room with a dirt floor and granite walls.

"It smells like an old, wet dog down here," said Mrs. Hornsbee.

There were shelves lined with mason jars, gray with dust. One corner was stacked with lobster traps. Googer shivered, remembering his dream.

"Well, I don't see our prankster," said Mrs. Hornsbee. "Let's go back upstairs. It's cold down here."

"Wait!" said Googer, pointing the light on a rotting workbench. "Look at that!"

There on the bench was an ancient fiddle, so covered with dust that it was obvious it hadn't been touched in years.

Mr. Hornsbee moved toward the workbench to examine the instrument, but before he could put his hand on it, the basement door slammed shut. Googer was so startled that he dropped the flashlight, plunging them into total darkness. Before anyone could react, the strange strains of fiddle music that had brought them to the basement in the first place began again.

"It's the g-g-ghost!"

"Mom?"

"I'm right here, Dalton. Jonathan, let's get out of here!"

"Wait a minute. I'm looking for the flashlight. I don't want any of you breaking your neck on those stairs."

"Mr. Hornsbee? I know this sounds crazy, but the music seems to be coming from *under* us."

"Maybe somebody's buried down there, Dad."

"No one is buried down there, and there is *no ghost*! Where is that flashlight?"

Suddenly a terrible voice echoed in the darkness: "All right. Who's down there?"

Everyone froze.

Mr. Orly Bean stood in the kitchen before the quartet like some medieval inquisitor. Neither Mr. nor Mrs. Hornsbee offered any explanation as to why they'd all been huddled in the pitch-black cellar when Bean opened the basement door. Orly explained that he had stopped by to see how they were doing and found the front door open but no one about. That was when he'd heard voices coming from the basement.

"Mr. Bean," said Mr. Hornsbee, "according to my cousin's will, if the nearest of kin, namely us, should decide not to accept Aloysius's estate, who would be next in line to inherit this place?"

Orly Bean's face remained stony, but he began to drum his fingers on the kitchen table. "Why, I would," he said.

"That's what I thought," replied Mr. Hornsbee.

It was evident to both Gitter and Googer that Mr. Hornsbee believed that Orly Bean was trying to scare them. If that were true, the boys reasoned, then two facts simply did not add up. First, the ghost they had seen looked exactly like the picture of Aloysius Hornsbee's grandfather and nothing at all like Orly Bean. Second, their ghost had disappeared into thin air. How could Orly Bean have done that?

"Nope," mused Gitter, "I think we have ourselves a real, live ghost."

Later that day Gitter and Googer wandered down to the harbor in search of Benjamin Whittle. Googer still had misgivings about Benjamin, but he also had a feeling that the lobsterman just might know something about their ghost.

Whittle, as promised, was working on his boat.

"Welcome aboard, boys," he said as he gave them a hand on board. "You're just in time to help me swab the deck. Then I'll be finished."

When the deck was shining and the boys had been given a full tour of the *Red Rigger*, Benjamin offered to treat them to a soda. The trio strolled up the street to Jane's Cafe and settled into a booth.

"Hear you've been having quite a time

up at the Hornsbee place," said Benjamin. "Ghosts, is it?"

"How did you know?" Googer asked.

"Ran into Orly Bean at lunch."

"Have you ever heard of ghosts up there before? Did Cousin Aloysius ever talk about them?" Gitter asked.

"Nope. Can't say as he ever did."

"Mom and Dad don't believe it's a ghost. Dad thinks it's Orly Bean."

"It's not Orly."

"How do you know?" asked Googer.

"Just know, that's all."

"We don't think it's Orly Bean either," Gitter confided. "The trouble is how to prove it."

"Catch the ghost," said Benjamin Whittle.

"Right," said Googer. "But how?"

Benjamin grinned. "You'll come up with a way, I bet. May not be as hard as you think."

"I still think he knows something he's not telling," said Googer on their way home.

"Maybe," Gitter agreed, "but I like him."

"Yeah, so do I," said Googer.

Suddenly Gitter leaped into the air and with a loud war whoop raced off toward the house. "Googer, Googer, Googer!" he hollered back over his shoulder as his friend ran to catch up. "You and I," he stopped and stated firmly, "are about to catch us a ghost!"

Chapter Eight

The ghost trap was an elaborate set-up, with wires and trips and alarms carefully placed about Gitter and Googer's bedroom. The boys figured that the ghost would almost certainly appear in their bedroom again. They knew from their winter research that ghosts had a habit of returning to the scene of the crime.

They attached one end of a wire to the bedroom doorknob and the other end to the switch of Googer's "Simon Says" computerized word game, which they placed on the desk. When the door was opened, the switch to the battery-operated computer would turn on and Simon's voice would alert the boys, even if they were asleep, to someone's presence. Gitter was delighted to find such an inspired use for "Stupid Simon," as he called the game. He would never have brought it at all, but spelling was one of his weak spots, and Mr. Hornsbee was determined to strengthen it.

If the first trap failed, another wire was stretched across the room from wall to wall just three feet in front of the door. Anyone touching that wire would cause an old coat rack, which the boys had loaded with pots and pans and tin cans, to come crashing to the floor with a clatter loud enough to wake the dead.

Above all of this, suspended from the ceiling in the center of the room, Gitter and Googer had rigged a small platform on which sat a pail of white paint they had found in the garage. A light rope was tied to the platform and stretched to a spot between the boys' beds. One good pull on the rope and anyone who stood underneath the paint would be white-washed from head to toe.

Now what the boys *really* hoped to prove with all of this equipment was that their night visitor *was* a ghost. If Aloysius Hornsbee's grandfather truly walked the floors of this house, then none of the traps would work. A ghost who walked through walls and could disappear at will would certainly walk right through the wire traps and in no way be affected by the paint—absolute proof of its spirituality. That fact, the boys felt, would be ample evidence that Mr. Orly Bean was not the ghost of the Hornsbee house, in spite of what the Gitter's parents thought.

To ensure no human participation other than their own, Googer fashioned a sign which he taped outside their bedroom door. It read, "Caution—Ghost Trap In Operation."

Gitter and Googer stayed awake as long

as they could that night—well past midnight, the hour any respectable ghost would appear—but to no avail. No ghost showed up, at least not while Gitter and Googer were conscious. The second night was equally unsuccessful. On the third night the stars shone brightly and the moon hung like an ornament in the black sky. In its own quiet way, this night was as spooky as the stormy one a few nights earlier.

Gitter was propped up in bed, his eyelids growing heavy, while Googer rested his elbows on the sill of the open window and looked out into the night. The reflection of the moon on the surf below was bright enough to illuminate the shape of a large ship slowly making its way up the coast at least half a mile out to sea.

"Hey, Gitter," Googer said, breaking long minutes of quiet.

"Mmmm?"

"There's someone walking by the rocks down at the beach. I can see him."

"Mmmm."

"Wake up," Googer pleaded. "Come here and look."

Gitter reluctantly got out of bed and looked out the window. Sure enough, there was a figure moving slowly among the rocks along the shore. Gitter couldn't make out if it was a man or a woman, but it definitely was real.

"I sure wish we hadn't left that spyglass in the tree," he said.

"Hey, Mister," Googer suddenly shouted out the window at the top of his lungs. "Getting any fish?"

"Will you be quiet," Gitter hissed. "Do you want to wake my mom and dad and have them come in here and set off the traps?"

"I was just having some fun. We've been waiting for this ghost for three nights. Hey, maybe that isn't a man down there—maybe it's the Windingo?"

"The what?"

"The Windingo! You know, the horrible

creature Mr. Bean said was known to roam this part of the state." The Googer furrowed his eyebrows and squinted his eyes. "They say it stands up like a man but has hair all over its body and huge, buggy eyes and snapping claws like a lobster instead of hands. It scares little kids to death, then uses them for bait in its lobster traps."

Gitter laughed. "Mr. Bean didn't say that. You made it up."

"I know." Googer laughed back, then added in a mock serious voice, "But the Windingo will get you if you don't watch out." He would have leaped on Gitter and wrestled with him if he hadn't been afraid of setting off the traps.

Before much longer the Windingo, the ghost traps, Mr. Orly Bean, and even the ghost were forgotten, and Gitter and Googer were sound asleep.

Perhaps an hour later a loud "thunk" caused the Googer to stir a bit and half awaken. His eyelids fluttered, then slowly came open. Standing before him was the bizarre figure of the Hornsbee ancestor swaying to and fro just a few feet away from the beds. Strange whispering sounds came from its lips. None of the traps had been triggered.

The Googer tried to call out, but his voice stuck in his throat. He pulled his gaze from the ghost to the Gitter's bed, making odd croaks in his attempts to speak. When he inched his head around again, the ghost was gone.

"Gitter!" he hollered. "Get up! It's the ghost."

Gitter came awake with a start and sat up in his bed. "What? Who? Where?"

"The ghost was standing right there just a minute ago. It was awful. But it disappeared before I could wake you up."

"Thunk," came a sound from the closet.

"I think . . . I think it's in there," Gitter said, pointing to the closet door.

Gitter and Googer looked at each other

and slowly nodded their heads. They got out of their beds and tiptoed carefully across the floor, avoiding the traps. Googer was in the lead. When they reached the closet, they paused and stared at each other. In another second they would be face to face with a ghost. Then Googer swallowed hard and gave a quick yank on the closet door.

The door swung open so easily that Googer lost his balance, falling backward into Gitter. The boys crashed to the floor in a tangle of arms and legs and set off all the traps. "Crash! Bang! Clang! Whomp! ... Simon says, spell ghost, g-h-o-s-t, ghost ... Ahhh, Ouch! Ow! ... Simon says, spell ghastly, g-h-a-s-t-l-y ... Oh, no!" The two figures in the middle of the floor were suddenly covered with a thick coat of white paint, making them look as ghostly as ...

But the closet was empty.

Chapter Nine

Dalton Hornsbee and Prentiss Luggs were not the most popular boys in Moody, Maine, that misty Thursday morning—at least not with Mr. and Mrs. Hornsbee. It had taken over an hour to clean up the boys (the paint they had found was not water soluble) and now they were confined to their room until the last remnants of the ghost trap were cleaned away.

Gitter and Googer had felt pretty silly when the Gitter's parents found them covered with paint in the middle of the night, but on the whole they thought it was worth the embarrassment. After all, they *had* proved that the creature was a ghost. Of course, they hadn't yet convinced Mr. and Mrs. Hornsbee, but they were working on that.

Jonathan Hornsbee was repairing a couple of broken shutters when a man appeared in the yard behind him.

"Mr. Hornsbee?" a full, deep voice inquired.

Jonathan jumped. "Yes," he answered the weathered stranger.

"I know yuh boys," Benjamin Whittle said very slowly.

Mr. Hornsbee glanced up to the boys' bedroom window, wondering what additional mischief they had been up to. "Dalton and Prentiss are under my care," he said cautiously.

"Yuh mean Gitter and Googer, don't yuh?"

Mr. Hornsbee laughed. "Yes, Gitter and Googer. Anything wrong?"

"Not that I know of," said the man.

"Then, what can I do for you?"

"I'm a lobsterman, and I've seen yuh boys down at the harbor. I thought they might like to come out on the boat with me this afternoon."

"Well, that's very kind of you, Mr. . . ."

"Whittle. Benjamin Whittle," the lobsterman said and accepted Mr. Hornsbee's offer of a handshake. "If yuh boys could be at the harbor by four o'clock, I'll have them home by seven."

"Mr. Whittle, I don't even know. . ."

"Thar could be some weather," Whittle interrupted as he looked up at the sky. "Better rig Gitter and Googer with some rain gear. If yuh don't have any, there's some in yuh garage."

Mr. Hornsbee looked at the strange man incredulously. How did he know there was rain gear in the garage?

"I, uh. . . yuh cousin Aloysius and I were friends," Whittle answered Mr. Hornsbee's question before he had a chance to ask it. "It's my duty to be hospitable to his kin," he said and turned to walk out of the yard.

Before Mr. Hornsbee could stop him, a car pulled into the long driveway. It was Ken Ashton, Orly Bean's assistant.

"Hello, Benjamin!" Ashton called out his car window as he drove past the lobsterman. Whittle raised his arm in a gesture of acknowledgment and continued to walk down the driveway.

Ken and Jonathan exchanged pleasantries, then Ken offered some information about Benjamin Whittle.

"He's a good man, Mr. Hornsbee, and one of the best fishermen in a town full of them. The boys will be in good hands."

"How did you know he wanted to take the boys out?" Mr. Hornsbee asked him.

Ken grinned. "Mr. Hornsbee, the Down Easters in this little town know just about everything about everybody. They know one another so well that they don't even have to tell one another what they're up to. It took me awhile to get used to it too, but you'll get the hang of it before long. At any rate, I just stopped by to give you this." He took an envelope from his pocket and handed it to Mr. Hornsbee. "Mr. Bean wanted me to make sure you got this," he said and turned back to his car. "Hope your boys enjoy the day," he added and then was gone.

Mr. Hornsbee was joined in the yard by his wife. He told her of the two visits, then opened the envelope from Mr. Bean and carefully read its contents.

"What is it, Jonathan?"

"Well, I'll be," Mr. Hornsbee said. "It's an official disclaimer from Orly Bean on inheriting this property."

"What does that mean?"

"It means," Mr. Hornsbee said with a frown, "that Orly Bean will gain nothing if we lose Aloysius's estate. It's his way of telling us that he is definitely *not* our ghost."

"Oh, dear," sighed Mrs. Hornsbee.

Chapter Ten

"Time you just called me Benjamin," the captain and owner of the *Red Rigger* told Gitter and Googer. He then proceeded to school them in the safety rules and regulations they would follow while aboard the small fishing vessel. A thrill of anticipation ran through them when Benjamin finally started the inboard motor and eased the *Red Rigger* through the harbor and out to sea.

It was cool and misty on the water, and the boys were glad to be wearing slickers. Gitter's mackintosh was the one Googer had given him before they left Minnesota, but Googer's slick, yellow, rubber gear had been found in the garage, and even with the sleeves rolled up, it was comically oversized.

Enroute to the place where Benjamin had set his lobster pots, as he called the traps, he let the boys take turns at the wheel in the crowded, little cabin.

"Two degrees starboard," Benjamin instructed Googer and watched as the boy inched the wheel slightly to the right. The *Red Rigger* obeyed, slapping its way across the choppy sea, up and down, up and down. Gitter and Googer were too excited to think about getting seasick.

"Buoys off the port bow," Benjamin noted, pointing ahead and to the left. "Put them there myself yesterday when I set my traps. Otherwise I'd never find 'em." Benjamin took over the wheel and brought the *Red Rigger* just a few feet from the markers, cut the engine, and showed Gitter how to "drop anchor."

For the next two hours Gitter and Googer

helped Benjamin pull in the lines with the lobster pots attached. He showed them how to open the traps and grab the crustaceans by the backs in order to avoid their snapping claws. The live lobsters were then thrown into the water-filled hold where they'd stay fresh on their way to market.

In the rare moments that Benjamin paused from his labor, he looked to the horizon for signs of a change in the weather. It had been misting ever since they left the harbor, but once they were working, the boys had hardly noticed the mist from above, they were so drenched by the never-ending spray from the ocean.

Then quite suddenly Benjamin called a halt to their activities. "Look down there," he said, pointing to the south.

"What is it?"

"A squall line...and coming in fast," he answered. "Ay-yup, we'd better pull up anchor and head back right away or you boys'll be wetter than muh lobsters."

In no time at all the gray skies began to blacken, and in the distance the boys could see sheets of rain falling. The sea was getting rougher too.

Benjamin paid little attention to Gitter and Googer as he secured the *Red Rigger* and pulled up anchor.

"Yuh best stay in the cabin now, boys. It looks as if we may be in for a rough one."

"Can we help you, Benjamin?" Googer asked.

"Ay-yup. You can help by sittin' back in that corner and keepin' tight. Cap'n Ben'll take care of the *Rigger* now."

Gitter and Googer felt the pulse of approaching danger and did as they were told. The *Red Rigger* began to roll harder. In a matter of seconds the wind was up to forty knots and the rain was coming down so hard that Gitter couldn't make out where it stopped and the ocean started. He'd never seen anything happen so fast in his life. He tried to say something to

Googer, but the combined roar of the feisty waters and the downpour of rain was joined by thunderous claps from the boiling sky, obliterating his voice.

Benjamin kept a steady hand at the helm as the *Rigger* met and conquered increasingly large and angry waves. The engine struggled against the rage of the storm, and the *Red Rigger* rocked precariously from port to starboard and from bow to stern as enormous waves crashed down on the cabin and deck.

Whittle's stoic face looked worried whenever he glanced back at the two small figures huddled in the cabin's corner. He reached for the *Rigger*'s radio, shouting into the microphone he held in one hand while the boat's engine sputtered in the violence of the storm. Gitter and Googer could barely make out his words, but they knew he was trying to give the Coast Guard their location.

Then, as quickly as the storm had set upon them, two things happened simultaneously that would seal the *Red Rigger*'s fate. The sputtering engine choked, coughed, and died as an angry wave rolled the *Rigger* close to capsizing. Benjamin Whittle careened against the cabin wall. The microphone, still in his hand, was torn from the transmitter.

The engine was out. The radio was out. The storm raged.

Benjamin motioned for the boys to come to the helm. "The engine's out," he screamed above the fury. "You boys'll have to take the wheel. Keep her starboard if yuh can. I've got to get the engine started again or we're in real trouble."

Gitter and Googer grimly followed instructions and grabbed the wheel.

"She'll buck yuh like crazy," boomed the big voice, "but if you can keep her starboard, we'll stay off the rocks."

Dalton Hornsbee and Prentiss Luggs gripped the spokes of the wheel and held on for dear life as Benjamin went aft in hopes of restarting the *Rigger*'s engine.

The wheel bucked and jerked in their hands, but they kept the *Red Rigger* pointed starboard and away from the rocks they knew were there but couldn't see.

For what seemed like hours Gitter and Googer held their post as the storm fought and roared and thundered about them. An occasional lightning flash confirmed the fact that they were dangerously close to the rocky coast. It seemed as if the boys could hear the engine sputter to life again when the wheel, with enormous force, spun out of their hands, and the *Red Rigger* lurched into the air on a gigantic wave and came pounding down on a strip of coastal rock. The *Rigger* had crashed.

The *Red Rigger,* its captain, and its crew were victims of a freak storm that threatened to make them statistics and the wild Atlantic Ocean their cold, wet grave.

Chapter Eleven

The wreckage of the *Red Rigger* was lodged between rocks on the rugged Maine coast. Huge chunks of wood had been wrenched from the starboard bow when the boat crashed.

Gitter came to in the little cabin, now leaning on its side. His head ached badly, but no bones seemed broken. The last thing he remembered was the wheel spinning out of their hands and the Googer and...Gitter looked about the cabin. The Googer was gone! He began to tremble as he considered the dreadful possibility that his friend had been washed overboard, but his fears were soon dispelled.

"Help! Gitter, help us!" came a cry from the deck of the *Red Rigger*. It was Googer's voice.

Gitter managed to crawl out the cabin door and onto the deck. The rain still slammed down on the beaten boat. Its precarious angle made movement difficult. The Googer was crouched over the prone captain who was lying under a portion of the fallen mast.

"Gitter," Googer cried, "help me get this off Benjamin's legs."

Whittle's pain was obvious despite the fact that he was trying not to show it. Gitter edged his way to Googer and Benjamin, and together the boys mustered unnatural strength and moved the broken mast off the injured man. Suddenly they heard a terrible "crack" above the howling storm and realized that what was left of the *Red Rigger* was about to break into pieces. They had to get off the boat *now*!

"Look," cried Gitter, pointing inland.

Through the rage of the storm they could see the outlines of the abandoned lighthouse—*their* lighthouse!

Gitter and Googer pulled Benjamin to the edge of the bow. A drop of several feet would put them safely on the ground—if they could get down before the *Rigger* broke up completely.

Benjamin could help himself a little, but his right leg was badly injured. "I'll lower you two down first," he told them. "Then you can help me." With a strength that astonished the boys, he lowered them from the side of the boat, then turned himself around and slid down to land with most of his weight on his left leg.

The lighthouse was only yards away, but it would be rough going over the ragged rocks through the pounding of the storm. If they were to be safe, though, they had to reach shelter. Otherwise they risked being washed out to sea.

Googer took Benjamin's left arm and Gitter took his right, but it was so dark they had trouble finding footing. Googer reached into the deep pocket of his oversized mackintosh and pulled out his Spiderman flashlight. The trio inched their way up and across the rocks toward the safety of the lighthouse.

They reached the flat land surrounding the lighthouse just as another wave hit the shore and ended the long life of the *Red Rigger*. Benjamin Whittle looked back at the shattered bit of wood and metal that had once been his boat. By morning even that would be gone.

The beam of Googer's flashlight dimly lit the musty-smelling room that was the first floor of the lighthouse. Gitter and Googer had eased Benjamin onto the floor and found some rags to serve as a pillow. His leg was bleeding badly. They couldn't wait out the storm—they had to get help *now*.

Benjamin was slipping in and out of consciousness and shivering from the rain and cold. "You boys are brave," he said, his voice strained. "We haven't been fair to you, and I want yuh to know about the...about the gho..." and he was out again.

"Before we go for help, let's see if we can find a cover for him," Googer said. He shined his light on the spiral stairs that led to the top of the lighthouse and began to climb. It seemed to take forever, but they finally reached the top. The huge arc light that had lit the nights for years was cold and dead, but through the windows from this vantage point they saw the storm still in full fury all around them.

Gitter and Googer found a blanket—and a bed, a table and chairs, and some personal items. Someone was living here at the top of the lighthouse, but the boys didn't even discuss the obvious—there was no time.

Near the top of the staircase Googer found what appeared to be an electric switch. "Maybe this'll turn the spot on," he said.

"No. This place has been abandoned for years," Gitter answered. Then both boys looked back on the portion of the room so clearly lived in. Googer couldn't resist a try and flipped the metal handle up.

"A-ooooooo, Ah, A-ooooooo, Ah." A deafening sound bellowed throughout the lighthouse. The boys nearly jumped out of their slickers.

"What on earth?" Gitter shouted, but his voice couldn't be heard. The fog horn filled the wild night. Perhaps it would bring help.

Googer led the way back downstairs. Gitter followed, laden with blankets. Two-thirds of the way down Googer stopped short and pointed to the floor below them. His face turned white and his legs began to shake. There in the beam from his Spiderman flashlight stood the ghost.

For one panicked moment the boys were paralyzed. They couldn't go back up—

they'd be trapped. Only one option remained—down the stairs, past the ghost, and out. And there was only one chance of making it. Googer said a silent prayer that ghosts' eyes were sensitive to light. Then he shined his flashlight directly into the ghost's face and made a dash for it. He could only hope that if it worked, Gitter would be right behind him.

Chapter Twelve

It did, and Gitter was. They tore down the beach toward the stairs to their house, but the ghost was in hot pursuit. Glancing back, Googer could see the huge figure, its arms waving menacingly in the air, its mouth open in what must have been some horrible growl, though he could hear nothing.

Closer and closer to safety they ran, and still the rain battered the coast and the wind blew up anything that wasn't tied down. Just as they reached the stairs that led up the side of the cliff to the Hornsbee property, Googer tripped on his long mackintosh and went flopping to the sand. He was up in a flash, but in the instant's pause in their escape that his fall had created, Gitter and Googer knew that their doom was sealed. The stairs up to the house were a shambles, another victim of the storm. The boys' hearts sank. Before either could think of what to do next, the ghost was upon them, one cold, wet arm around each of them.

Mr. and Mrs. Hornsbee, Orly Bean, and Kenneth Ashton were joined in the Hornsbee kitchen by two sheriff's deputies. The sheriff's men were in constant touch with the Coast Guard, but no trace of the *Red Rigger* had been found. They had done everything humanly possible after receiving the *Rigger*'s distress signal. In fact, everyone in Moody had offered their help. No one seemed more upset than Orly Bean.

"Mr. Hornsbee, Mrs. Hornsbee," Bean said with difficulty, "I know this isn't a good time, but I feel I must tell you something. I feel so terrible about those wonderful boys. . . ."

But before Orly could finish, Bob Holec, one of the deputies, was getting a garbled message on his two-way radio. He held it up to his ear while everyone else remained quiet for the news.

"Well, I'll be," he finally said.

"What is it, Mr. Holec?" asked Mrs. Hornsbee with hope in her voice.

"Sam and Elliot have just found Benjamin Whittle in the old lighthouse. That fog horn made them suspicious, and when they went in, they found him."

"Is he all right?" asked Mr. Hornsbee.

"Yes. He was unconscious, but they have him at County General and he'll be okay."

"What about Dalton and Prentiss?" Mrs. Hornsbee asked, holding back her tears.

"They're right here, Mrs. Hornsbee," said a strange voice.

Everone turned around. There in the open basement doorway stood the Gitter, the Googer, and the Ghost.

Epilogue

"It all started when my good friend Orly Bean insisted that I make out a will. . . ."

Aloysius P. Hornsbee sat in the Luggs' living room in Red Wing, Minnesota. It was Thanksgiving evening. The Luggs and the Hornsbee families had decided to celebrate the holiday together this year since they were feeling most thankful for the same thing: the return of Gitter and Googer.

Although everyone in the room had heard the story many times before, it was a treat to hear it directly "from the horse's mouth"—and the "horse" clearly loved to tell it.

"Trouble was, I didn't have anyone to leave my house *to.* Orly insisted that I must have some relatives somewhere, so he engaged young Ken Ashton to do some detective work. Waall, when I found out that I *did* have relatives, I still had a problem. Who were they? I knew their names then, of course—Jonathan, Cynthia, and Dalton Hornsbee—but who were they *really*? What were they like underneath? Blood relations or not, I just couldn't see clear to leaving the house that my grandfather had built with his own hands to strangers. No, I loved that house too much. So I decided to pretend I was dead."

"I still don't understand why you just didn't come out here and meet the Hornsbees," said Sally Luggs. "It would've been a whole lot simpler."

"Ay-yup, it would have," Aloysius agreed, "but there are two important things it wouldn't have told me. Remember, I didn't know Jonathan and Cynthia yet. If they'd turned out to be greedy people, they might have been good to me just so they'd inherit the property. Besides, I wanted to see my heirs *in* my house. I wanted to make sure that they would love and care for it."

"Tell about how you pretended to be a ghost!" Googer's littlest brother, Arthur, demanded.

"Waall now, Arthur, I *didn't* pretend to be a ghost—at least not at first. Then the night that the boys caught me in their room, I hid in their closet and listened to them tell Jonathan about this ghost that they'd just seen. Ay-yup, the boys were so serious, and they wanted a ghost so badly, I nearly burst out laughing right there in that closet. I decided then and there that it was high time I had a little fun. Ay-yup, I'd give them their ghost all right, and I'd have a much easier time keeping an eye on my kin in the process.

"Now, you have to know a little about my grandfather, Dalton Hornsbee, and the house that he built, before you can see just how easy it was for me to play ghost.

Grandfather Hornsbee built that house before the Civil War. It was a regular stop on the Underground Railway. Dalton Hornsbee hid runaway slaves who were on their way to freedom in Canada. He hid them in the room where Gitter and Googer here slept, but if someone came, he had to have a way to get them out without anyone seeing. So he built a secret door in the closet that opened onto a stairway leading straight down to the basement. There's a trapdoor down there, and a long rope ladder. Leads to a cave down on the beach. That's how the slaves escaped, and that's how I got Gitter and Googer up from the beach on the night of the storm. 'Course I didn't live in the cave. Lighthouse was a lot more cozy, and Ben Whittle kept me supplied with all I needed."

"There's more coffee if anyone would like some," Granny Goodwich said, coming in from the kitchen with a large plate of cookies, "and some chocolate chip cookies fresh from the oven too."

"Rita Luggs, you make the best darn chocolate chip cookies I ever ate."

"Why, thank you, Aloysius. Now finish your story or we'll never make that movie you promised me."

"Waall now, I think I've about finished it." He went to the closet to get his and Granny's coats. "I haven't been to the moving pictures since I was a youngster of about fifty."

"There's just one thing I don't get," said Googer in a puzzled tone of voice.

"What's that?"

"The day we found your old fiddle in the basement, it was all covered with dust. Did you have another one that you played?"

"Fiddle?" said Aloysius. "I don't play the fiddle. The one in the basement was Granddad's. Far as I know, nobody's played that fiddle or any other in the Hornsbee house since he died."

Gitter and Googer stared at each other.

"You mean . . ." said Gitter.

"There really *was* . . ." said Googer.

"Ay-yup," answered a soft voice.

The boys turned back to Aloysius, but he and Granny Goodwich were already out the door and on their way to the movie.

About the Author

Stephen Ryan Oliver grew up in Chippewa Falls, Wisconsin. He earned his B.A. in English and speech at the University of Wisconsin and participated in the graduate theater program at Hunter College in New York where he earned "a lot of headaches." At various times in his life Mr. Oliver has worked as an actor, a waiter, a singer, a dancer, and a teacher. He is currently a script writer in Los Angeles where he continues in his lifelong efforts to catch a ghost.